JE
Wax, Wendy
A royal Valentine

MID-CONTINENT PUBLIC LIBRARY
Parkville Branch
8815 N.W. 45 Highway
Parkville, MO 64152
PV

D0292879

by Wendy Wax
illustrated by Susan Hall

WITHDRAWN
FROM THE RECORDS OF THE
MID-CONTINENT PUBLIC LIBRARY

Ready-to-Read

SIMON SPOTLIGHT/NICKELODEON
New York London Toronto Sydney

MID-CONTINENT PUBLIC LIBRARY - INT
3 0007 00838006 4

Based on the TV series *Nick Jr. The Backyardigans*™ as seen on Nick Jr.®

SIMON SPOTLIGHT
An imprint of Simon & Schuster Children's Publishing Division
1230 Avenue of the Americas, New York, New York 10020
© 2006 Viacom International Inc. All rights reserved. NICK JR.,
Nick Jr. The Backyardigans, and all related titles, logos, and characters are trademarks of Viacom International Inc. All rights reserved, including the right of reproduction in whole or in part in any form.
SIMON SPOTLIGHT, READY-TO-READ, and colophon
are registered trademarks of Simon & Schuster, Inc.
Manufactured in the United States of America
4 6 8 10 9 7 5
Library of Congress Cataloging-in-Publication Data
Wax, Wendy.
A Royal Valentine / by Wendy Wax; illustrated by Susan Hall.—1st ed.
p. cm.—(Ready-to-read)
"Based on the TV series Nick Jr. The Backyardigans as seen on Nick Jr."
ISBN-13: 978-1-4169-0801-2 (pbk.)
ISBN-10: 1-4169-0801-3 (pbk.)
I. Hall, Susan, 1940- II. Title. III. Series.
PZ7.W35117Roy 2006
[E]—dc22
2005012110

Meet Queen !

TASHA

MID-CONTINENT PUBLIC LIBRARY
Parkville Branch
8815 N.W. 45 Highway
Parkville, MO 64152
PV

Queen  made a 

TASHA VALENTINE

for her best friend,

Queen  .

UNIQUA

TYRONE

and 
PABLO

will bring

the 
VALENTINE

to Queen 
UNIQUA

in her 
PALACE

far away.

"Nothing can stop us!"

says .

TYRONE

"Not , or ,

WIND SNOW

or the wide!"

RIVER

says.

PABLO

The blows.

WIND

"This is strong,"

WIND

says .

PABLO

" will not stop us!"
WIND
says .
TYRONE

SNOW starts to fall.

"SNOW will not stop us!"

says PABLO.

"I have .

GOGGLES

Now we can see the ."

PATH

"There is a wide ,"
RIVER
says .
PABLO
"How will we cross?"

"I know!" says.
TYRONE
"We will jump across on
the blocks of ."
ICE

"Nothing can stop us!" say
and .
PABLO
TYRONE
"Not , or , or the
WIND
SNOW
wide!"
RIVER

"Queen , here we
UNIQUA
come!" shouts .
TYRONE

At last  and 

TYRONE PABLO

reach the  .

PALACE

They knock on the  .

DOOR

"Who is there?" asks  ,

AUSTIN

the  guard.

PALACE

"Queen TASHA sent us,"

say PABLO and TYRONE.

"Come in," says AUSTIN.

"Special delivery for
VALENTINE
Queen from Queen ,"
UNIQUA
TASHA
call and .
PABLO
TYRONE

"Wow!" says Queen UNIQUA.

"I love it!

I have something

for Queen TASHA, too."

"We will bring it to her,"

says.

TYRONE

"Nothing can stop us!"

says .

PABLO

"I must give it to

Queen  myself,"

TASHA

says Queen  .

UNIQUA

"I want to go too!"  says.

AUSTIN

Queen ,
UNIQUA
, , and
AUSTIN
PABLO
TYRONE
go to see Queen .
TASHA

"Special delivery for

Queen 
TASHA
,"

says Queen 
UNIQUA
.

"What is it?" asks

Queen 
TASHA
.

"It is a big hug.

Happy Valentine's Day!"